Introducing Pop Monsters...

Deep in the heart of the Pacific Northwest there lives a furry band of critters that come in all shapes and sizes. In that wooded glen, among the misty meadows and mossy-bearded trees, they share fun and adventure in a magical place called Wetmore Forest.

STERLING CHILDREN'S BOOKS
New York

An Imprint of Sterling Publishing Co., Inc.
1166 Avenue of the Americas
New York, NY 10036

TUMBLEBEE
GOES FOR A WALK

A
WETMORE FOREST
STORY

By Randy Harvey and Sean Wilkinson
Illustrated by John Skewes

STERLING CHILDREN'S BOOKS
New York

One day in Wetmore Forest, Tumblebee decided to go for a walk. He had many favorite places in the forest where he liked to sit and think and daydream. But today, he had a very special place in mind.

It was a sunny little glen right on the banks of Silver Tree Creek, with tall grass and a perfect rock for sitting. Tumblebee knew just how to get there.

First, you took the water taxi across Forktail Creek.
That meant you got to say "Good Morning" to Smoots
and his loyal slog, Bickle.

Once across the creek, it was a nice, easy stroll through Breezly Fields, where Chitter-chat birds sang their cheerful little morning song from high up in the trees.

From there he followed the
trail down Zigzag Hill.

The steep hill could be slow going for
most, but not for Tumblebee! He did
what he did best: rolled up in a ball
and tumbled down the twisting trail!

He was almost at his
favorite thinking spot.

But when he finally got there,
Tumblebee was surprised to see that someone else
was already sitting on his special rock!

It was a monster that Tumblebee had never
seen before, right there in his spot.
Tumblebee approached the monster hesitantly.

"Hello,"

he said.

"Go away,"

the monster said.

Tumblebee was confused. He always liked to meet new monsters. Didn't everyone?

He tried to explain that this was his favorite rock in all of Wetmore Forest and he was happy to share. He would just sit quietly nearby if that was okay.

But the grouchy little monster wasn't having it. "It's my spot today," he said. "You can come back tomorrow. I just want to be left alone."

Tumblebee wasn't sure what to do. The little monster seemed angry... or sad. *Maybe he just needs a snack!* Tumblebee thought. He knew that sometimes when he got really hungry, it put him in a grouchy mood.

He ran off in search of a snack and soon returned with an armful of delicious Sneeze-wheezies.

"I don't want any. I'm not hungry."

Or maybe he needed cheering up.

Tumblebee snuck away quietly
to a nearby field and picked a
beautiful wildflower.

He brought it to the little monster and presented
his small gift. But the monster only scowled.

Maybe he needs to laugh,
Tumblebee thought.

He'd heard that laughter was good for the soul. So he went into the small grove of trees and thought up a funny little song and dance. He came back and performed it for the little monster.

"Fine, fine," the monster said. "You've done your dance. You can go now."

Well, Tumblebee was all out of ideas. It seemed like there wasn't anything that he could do to cheer the monster up! He sat by the river's edge, head in hands.

"Look," the monster said. "You seem okay. But I'm afraid you're going to be just like everyone else I've met here. No one wants to be my friend.

The fish won't swim with me because they say I'm too slow. The birds don't like my singing, and the beavers are too good for everybody. So I'm just going to be alone."

Tumblebee nodded, finally understanding why the monster was so sad. *Friends*, Tumblebee thought, *this little monster needs friends!*

Just then, a little butterfly landed on Tumblebee's nose.
This gave him an idea.

Tumblebee whispered a special message to the butterfly.

And after that day,
the little monster was never lonely again.

Collect all of the

WETMORE FOREST

Adventures.

Available now:

Coming Soon!